APR 8 8

KN

Spring Planting

By Rita Kohn

Illustrated by Robin McBride Scott

The Woodland Adventures series
is dedicated to all The Woodland People
who persevere despite hardships, inhumanity, and hostility.
Their spirit, like the Eagle, soars.
Their integrity, like the Turtle, persists.

This book is dedicated to
Michelle, Rosemary, Gwen, Lora,
Linda, Mike, Nick, and the memory of Chief Ray White,
whose seeds grow to cover much ground.

Special thanks to:
Wap Shing, spiritual Leader of the Miami of Indiana,
and to my Consultants
Curtis Zunigha - Lenape (Delaware) and Isleta Pueblo,
Rosemary Dougherty - Cherokee-Ojibwa; Associate Editor, *The Gourd Magazine*
and Beth Kohn - Early Childhood Specialist

Kohn, Rita T.
    Spring planting / by Rita Kohn; illustrated by Robin McBride Scott.
        p. cm. - (Woodland adventures)

    ISBN 0-516-05203-9

    1. Miami Indians -- Social life and customs -- Juvenile literature.
2. Spring -- Great Lakes Region -- Juvenile literature. [1. Miami Indians-
-Social life and customs. 2. Indians of North America -- Great Lakes
Region -- Social life and customs. 3. Spring. 4. Gourds.]
I. Scott, Robin McBride, ill. II. Title. III. Series.
E99.M48K65 1995
635'.61 --dc20   94-38377
                                                          CIP
                                                          AC

Project Editor: Alice Flanagan
Design and Electronic Production:
    PCI Design Group, San Antonio, Texas
Engraver: Liberty Photoengravers
Printer: Lake Book Manufacturing, Inc.

1 2 3 4 5 6 7 8 9 10 R 04 03 02 01 00 99 98 97 96 95

The Purpose of This Book

Spring Planting, one of four books having a SEASONAL theme in the Woodland Adventures series, is a picture book for preschool and primary grades based on learning number concepts such as SPATIAL RELATIONSHIPS, LINEAR MEASUREMENTS, and TIME MEASUREMENTS in months.

The story takes place in the spring in a woodland region along the Great Lakes of North America, the traditional homeland for more than twenty NATIVE AMERICAN nations. It focuses on a contemporary family of the Miami of Indiana and the traditional custom of planting gourds for the fall gathering give-away. By learning how to measure space for a garden and how to determine the length of growing time, readers will come to understand the life cycle from seed to plant and learn the significance of caring for living things and sharing them with others.

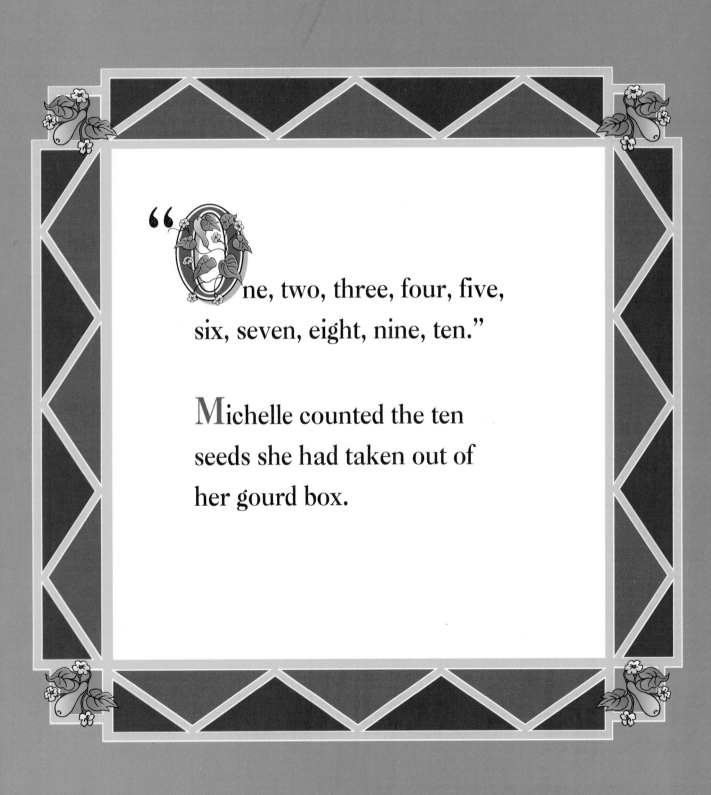

"One, two, three, four, five, six, seven, eight, nine, ten."

Michelle counted the ten seeds she had taken out of her gourd box.

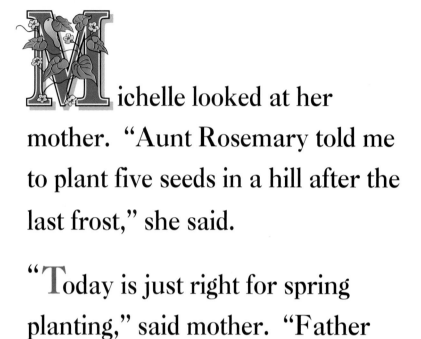

ichelle looked at her mother. "Aunt Rosemary told me to plant five seeds in a hill after the last frost," she said.

"Today is just right for spring planting," said mother. "Father and I will help you plant your seeds before we plant our own."

"It looks like we will need a larger garden than the one we had last year," said father.

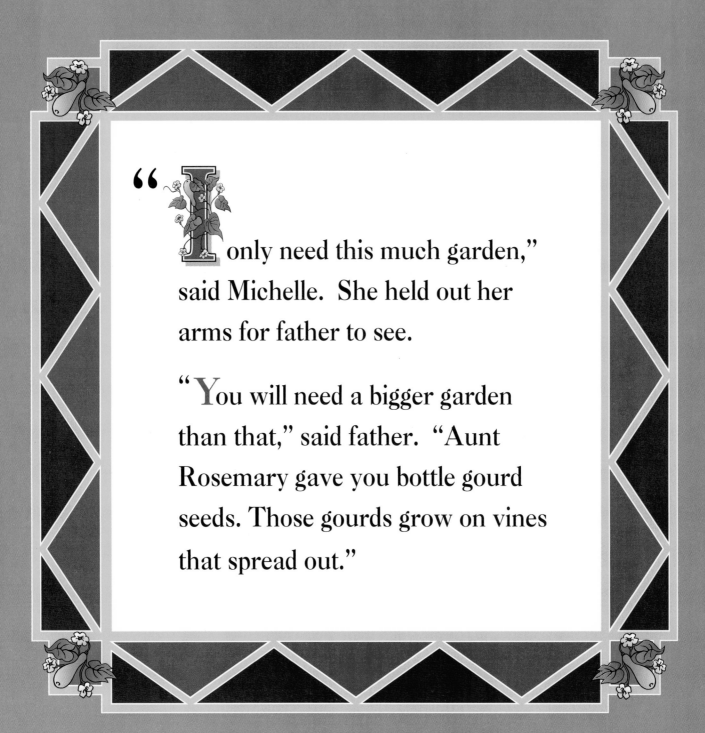

"I only need this much garden," said Michelle. She held out her arms for father to see.

"You will need a bigger garden than that," said father. "Aunt Rosemary gave you bottle gourd seeds. Those gourds grow on vines that spread out."

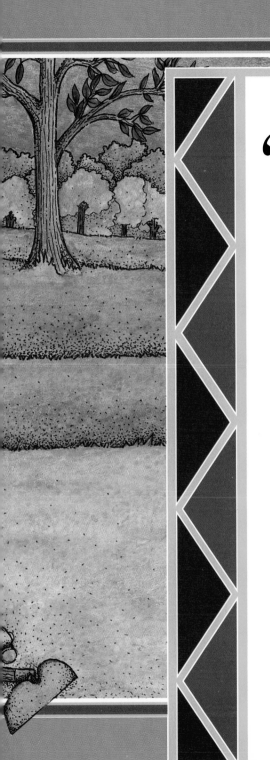

"Let's mark a sunny place for you to plant your seeds," said father.

He took the yardstick from the basket of tools and placed it on the ground. He drove stakes into the ground at each end of the yardstick.

JUNE						
				1	2	3
4	5	6	7	8	9	10
11	12	13	14	15	16	17
18	19	20	21	22	23	24
25	26	27	28	29	30	

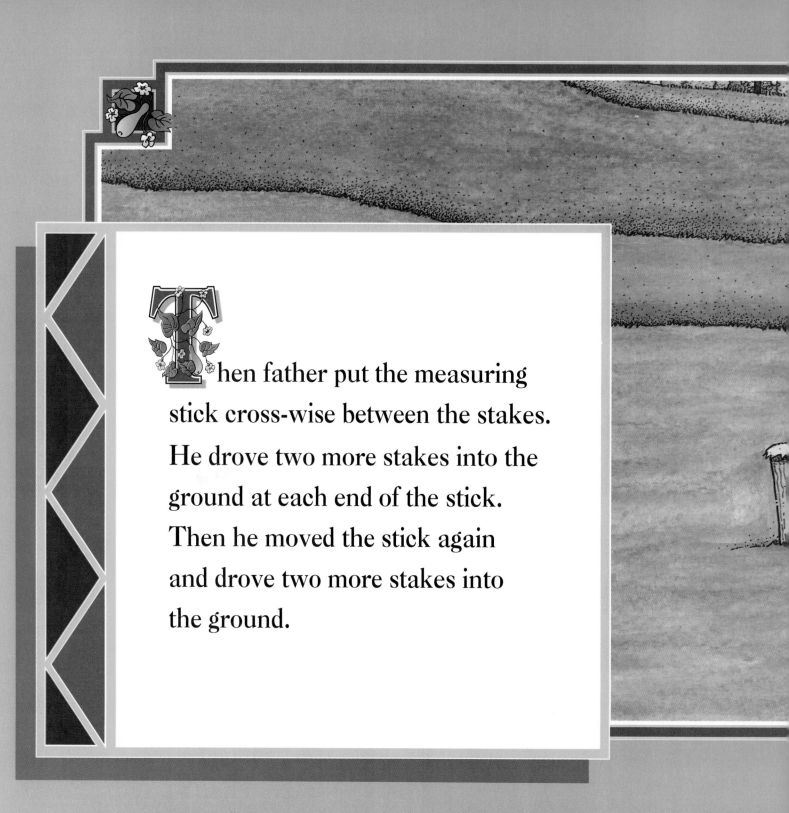

Then father put the measuring stick cross-wise between the stakes. He drove two more stakes into the ground at each end of the stick. Then he moved the stick again and drove two more stakes into the ground.

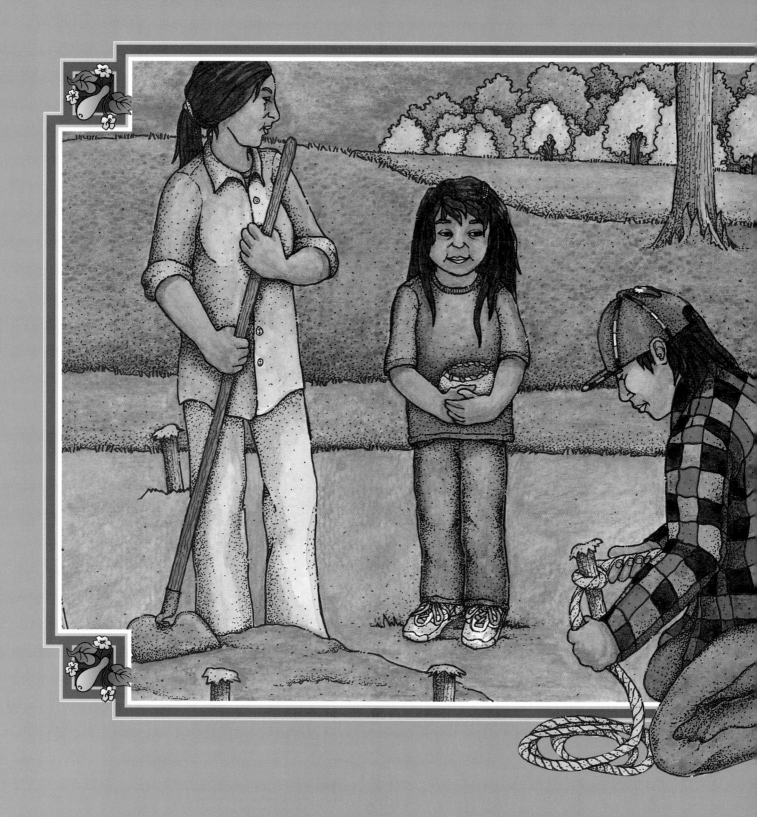

14

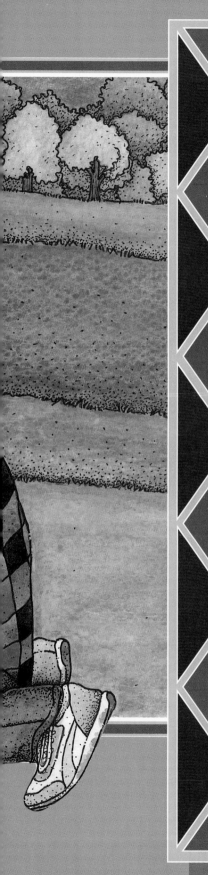

hen he did the same thing again in a spot next to the six stakes. Michelle watched. She held tightly to her gourd box with the seeds.

Father looped rope around the stakes. Mother used a garden hoe to make a hill of soft soil in the center of each circle.

"Plant your seeds in each hill," she said. "We will ask Mother Earth to keep them safe and help them grow so you will have many gourds to share with others."

"My little seeds will be lonely in this big place," said Michelle. "I will just hold them in my hands."

"Your seeds cannot grow if you just hold them in your hands," said mother. "Plant your seeds today," she said. "In ten days you will see tiny, green shoots coming up from the hills, just like in Aunt Rosemary's garden."

"Leaves will open up on the plants before the next full moon," said father. "It will be July. The hot sun will help your seeds make healthy plants, just like in Aunt Rosemary's garden."

JULY

						1
2	3	4	5	6	7	8
9	10	11	12	13	14	15
16	17	18	19	20	21	22
23	24	25	26	27	28	29
30	31					

"The vines will stretch out along the ground away from the hills of seeds," said mother. "Flowers will bloom along the vines. In August, bees will fly from flower to flower. They will pollinate the flowers so the gourds can grow on the vines, just like in Aunt Rosemary's garden."

AUGUST					
	1	2	3	4	5
6	7	8	9	10	11	12
13	14	15	16	17	18	19
20	21	22	23	24	25	26
27	28	29	30	31		

21

22

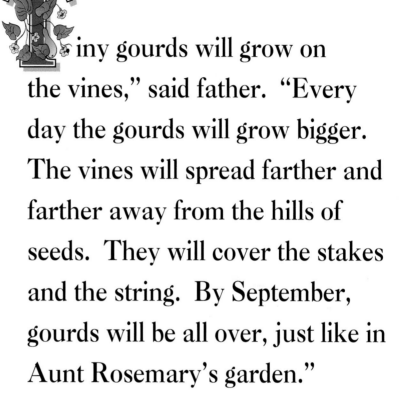

"Tiny gourds will grow on the vines," said father. "Every day the gourds will grow bigger. The vines will spread farther and farther away from the hills of seeds. They will cover the stakes and the string. By September, gourds will be all over, just like in Aunt Rosemary's garden."

SEPTEMBER						
					1	2
3	4	5	6	7	8	9
10	11	12	13	14	15	16
17	18	19	20	21	22	23
24	25	26	27	28	29	30

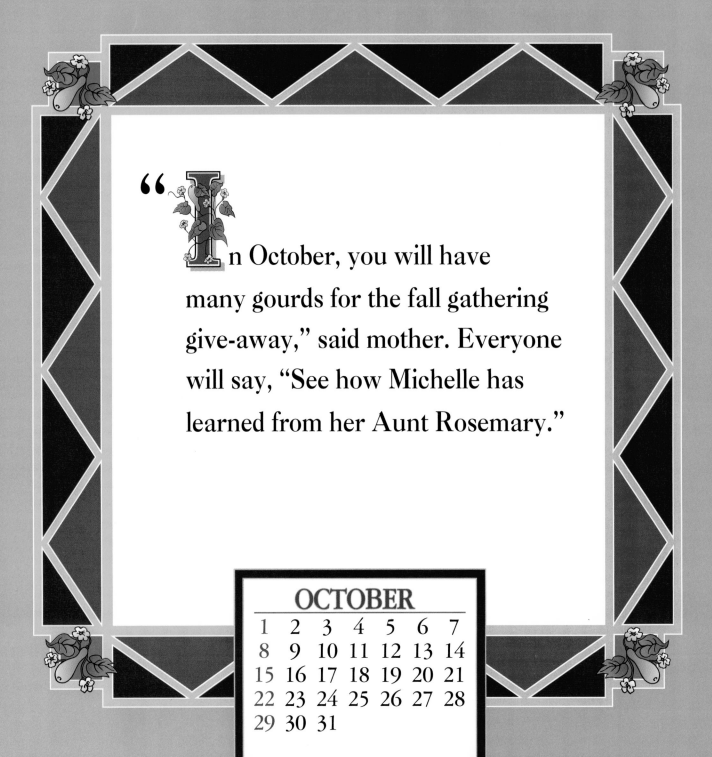

"In October, you will have many gourds for the fall gathering give-away," said mother. Everyone will say, "See how Michelle has learned from her Aunt Rosemary."

OCTOBER

1	2	3	4	5	6	7
8	9	10	11	12	13	14
15	16	17	18	19	20	21
22	23	24	25	26	27	28
29	30	31				

25

"Michelle smiled. Carefully, she placed five seeds in each hill. She covered them with soil and said, "Mother Earth, please help my little seeds grow."

Then Michelle thought, "Soon I will have many gourds for the fall gathering give-away. I will take the seeds from my own gourds. I will put them away in my gourd box and plant them next year. Aunt Rosemary will be proud of me."

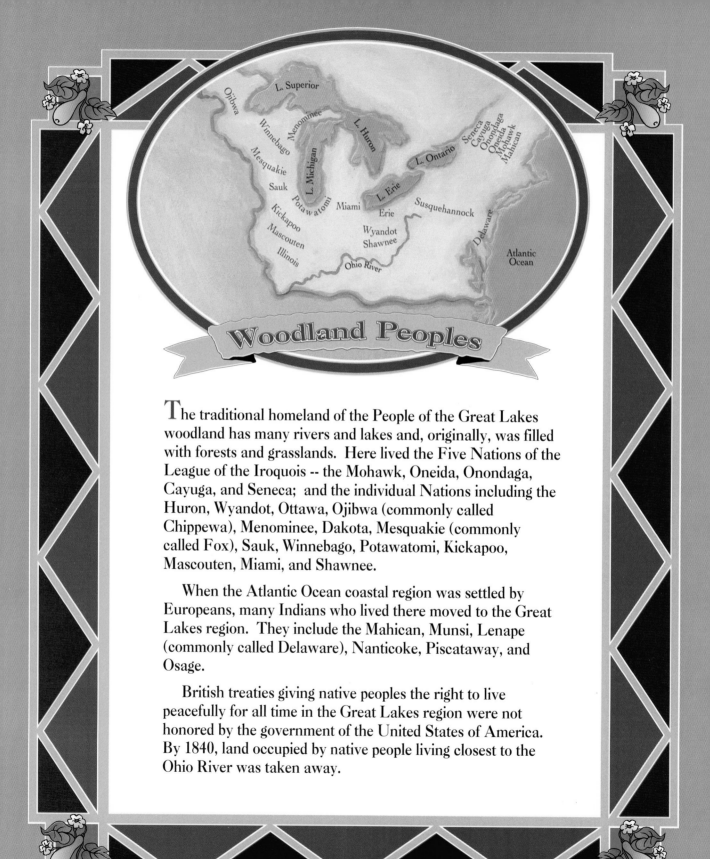

Woodland Peoples

The traditional homeland of the People of the Great Lakes woodland has many rivers and lakes and, originally, was filled with forests and grasslands. Here lived the Five Nations of the League of the Iroquois -- the Mohawk, Oneida, Onondaga, Cayuga, and Seneca; and the individual Nations including the Huron, Wyandot, Ottawa, Ojibwa (commonly called Chippewa), Menominee, Dakota, Mesquakie (commonly called Fox), Sauk, Winnebago, Potawatomi, Kickapoo, Mascouten, Miami, and Shawnee.

When the Atlantic Ocean coastal region was settled by Europeans, many Indians who lived there moved to the Great Lakes region. They include the Mahican, Munsi, Lenape (commonly called Delaware), Nanticoke, Piscataway, and Osage.

British treaties giving native peoples the right to live peacefully for all time in the Great Lakes region were not honored by the government of the United States of America. By 1840, land occupied by native people living closest to the Ohio River was taken away.

Planting Gourds

Gourds are part of a group of annual plants that grow on vines. The group includes cucumbers, melons, pumpkins, and squash. They are called annuals because they must be planted each year. Unlike other vine crops, gourds are not planted for food, but for ornamental use.

Gourds are often named for their shape. "Spoon" gourds take up less space than do "bottle" gourds, and the small spoon gourds are easy to handle for beginning crafts projects. Spoon gourd seed packets can be purchased from garden shops or ordered directly from: *Stokes Seeds, Inc., P.O. Box 548, Buffalo, NY 14240* or *R. H. Shumway, P.O. Box 1, Graniteville, SC 29829.*

Plant and harvest gourds according to the directions on the seed packets. Sow seeds outdoors after the soil warms. Generally, the seeds need temperatures of 60 to 75 degrees Fahrenheit, a lot of sunshine, and daily watering. Plant four or five spoon gourd seeds about one-half inch deep in a well-composed hill. Tamp the soil lightly. Water daily. In five to fifteen days, when the seedlings have two or three leaves, remove all but one or two large, healthy, well-spaced plants per hill. To keep the roots well irrigated, dig a trench around the hill and fill it with water. Avoid watering the plant from the top. Wet leaves often get diseases that cause the plant to die.

For the best gourds, allow the vines to grow on a trellis, fence, or pole. Let gourds ripen on the vine, and harvest just before the first frost. It takes ninety days (about three months) for gourds to be fully mature. Do not pick gourds too early.

Making Things

 fter you harvest fully mature gourds, wash each carefully in warm, sudsy water. Rinse and allow them to dry in a well-ventilated area. You might also apply floor wax and polish.

Use your imagination to make all sorts of things from the gourds.

1. Apply stick-on letters and pictures to gourds to make unique place cards and favors for a party. Send out invitations having the same stick-on letters and pictures that you have placed on the gourds. Ask your guests to bring their invitations to the party. Then have them locate their placement at the table by matching their invitations with the gourds.

2. To make centerpieces, arrange gourds with pine cones in a basket or bowl. Add dried leaves, flowers, and herbs, polished pebbles, and driftwood.

With Gourds

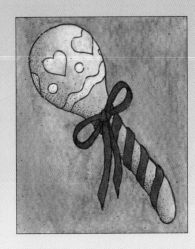

To make Halloween or Thanksgiving wall hangings or Christmas tree decorations, artfully tie or weave a net of string, yarn, and/or ribbons around gourds. Add feathers and strings of beads. To make wreaths, attach decorated gourds to a circle made from bent twigs or a clothes hanger wrapped with bright yarn or ribbon.

4. Make a gourd sculpture by gluing gourds together. Paint or decorate your own sculpture.

5. Making a baby rattle is simple and safe. Use only a spoon gourd dry enough to rattle. Make sure the handle is straight or easy to grasp. Wash it thoroughly in dish soap and hot water. Remove any dirt or mold. Let it dry. Tie a ribbon around the handle and give as a gift. This rattle is sturdy, washable, and not dangerous to children in any way.

About the Author

Rita Kohn grew up in the Catskill Mountains, went to college in Buffalo, New York, and now calls both Illinois and Indiana home. All these places are part of the ancestral territory of the Woodland People. A lifelong love of the land and the People whose spirit continues to give energy to these mountains, valleys, streams, lakes, and fields leads her to listen, watch, and learn. Her book is one way of continuing the circle of life.

About the Illustrator

Robin McBride Scott is of Irish, German, and Cherokee descent and adopted Osage. At the age of six, she learned beadwork from her maternal grandmother and began developing an interest in traditional arts and culture. Her love of art eventually led to a Bachelor of Fine Arts degree in graphic design from Ball State University in Muncie, Indiana, where she also received a minor in Metalsmithing and a minor in Native American Studies. Robin's main focus has been on the traditional arts of quillwork, beadwork, ribbonwork, clothing, and moccasin-making. Currently, however, she has been expanding her art form to include gourdwork and illustrations.